MW01601369

POND WATER GENESIS

BRENDA FIREEAGLE BIDDIX
RIAN MILETI

DISCLAIMER: THIS DOCUMENT IS A WORK OF FICTION. NAMES, CHARACTERS, BUSINESSES, PLACES, EVENTS, LOCALES, AND INCIDENTS ARE EITHER THE PRODUCTS OF THE AUTHOR'S IMAGINATION OR USED IN A FICTITIOUS MANNER. ANY RESEMBLANCE TO ACTUAL PERSONS, LIVING OR DEAD, OR ACTUAL EVENTS IS PURELY COINCIDENTAL.

COPYRIGHT © 2024 RIAN MILETI INVESTMENTS, LLC

Copyright Ownership: The work titled "Pond Water Genesis" is the intellectual property of Brenda (FireEagle) Biddix and Rian Mileti, copyrighted by Rian Mileti Investments LLC. Unauthorized use, reproduction, distribution, or modification of this work is strictly prohibited.
License: This work is licensed under the Creative Commons Attribution-NonCommercial-NoDerivatives 4.0 International License. To view a copy of this license, visit http://creativecommons.org/licenses/by-nc-nd/4.0/ or send a letter to Creative Commons, PO Box 1866, Mountain View, CA 94042, USA.

· **Non-Commercial Use:** You are permitted to share, copy, and redistribute the material in any medium or format under the following terms:
· **Attribution:** You must give appropriate credit to Brenda (FireEagle) Biddix and Rian Mileti, provide a link to the license, and indicate if changes were made. You may do so in any reasonable manner, but not in any way that suggests the licensor endorses you or your use.
· **NonCommercial:** You may not use the material for commercial purposes.
· **NoDerivatives:** If you remix, transform, or build upon the material, you may not distribute the modified material.

Inquiries: For inquiries regarding permissions beyond the scope of this license, please contact Rian Mileti Investments LLC.

Written by: Brenda (FireEagle) Biddix, Rian Mileti

THE AUTHORS

Brenda F. Biddix was born into the stark, natural beauty of an Appalachian hunting cabin in November 1950, marking the beginning of a life journey characterized by resilience, creativity, and profound change. With a degree from the Newspaper Institute of America, Brenda refined her craft in creative writing and expanded her expertise into psychiatric and clinical nursing, drawing deep insights into human resilience and the spirit. Despite a significant, life-altering accident in 1991, Brenda emerged as a relentless advocate within her church and community, fervently mentoring youth and combatting domestic violence. She poured her resilience into crafting *Inside The Pain: A Survivor's Guide to breaking the cycles of abuse and domestic violence.*

Her literary contributions have not gone unnoticed, earning her an Editor's Choice Award and a nomination for Poet of the Year in 2004 by the International Symposium of Poets. Brenda's eloquent words have been featured in *Lamplighter Magazine, Cherokee Sentinel, 'The Colors of Life,'* and *'Labyrinth of the Mind: A Poet's Muse.'* Facing Parkinson's Disease as a side-effect of arsenic poisoning presented a new challenge, but her spirit and creativity found new life. Thirteen years later, her desire to write was still alive even though Parkinson's became a huge barrier. Through doodles and descriptions, she developed the concept for *'Pond Water,'* and this thrilling sequel, *'Pond Water Riptide.'*

Rian Mileti, a devoted father and fierce friend, is the accomplished author of seven books, including the acclaimed *'The Color Gone.'* Known for his narrative prowess and humble demeanor, Rian prefers to let his storytelling capture the hearts and minds of his readers. He got his skills from his grandmother and best friend, Brenda.

Their collaborative efforts on *'Pond Water'* not only met but exceeded expectations, achieving #1 best-seller status on Amazon across multiple categories. *'Pond Water Riptide'* is not just a sequel but a continuation of their mission, carrying its hidden messages within its pages. The sales from these books directly support Brenda and others with Parkinson's by covering medical expenses and home modifications not covered by insurance. This initiative is a testament to their shared journey.

Thank you for being part of this meaningful journey. Your support makes a significant difference in the lives of those affected by Parkinson's Disease.

Below are some of her original sketches, which add depth to our shared experience. To avoid spoilers and enrich your understanding, a section titled **'The Silent Story'** has been added to the end of this book.

ADVENTURE
AWAITS

NEXT BOOK

SCAN ME

VISIT
RianMileti.com

Contents

EMERGENCE

"EVEN GOOD MEN meet their end," Ethan's voice echoed across the pond. It chilled the morning air. The revolver in his hand was steady, aimed right at Jared, its metal gleaming in the morning light.

Jared's heart pounded in his chest. "Ethan, I don't see how you can get out of this." Jared's voice strained with fear. He had faced death before, countless times, but this was different. This wasn't just about survival — it was about everything. The world outside faded, leaving only the sharp edge of Ethan's unflinching eyes.

Ethan's gaze was cold, calculating. Jared had seen that look before, years ago in the military. Back then, Ethan was precise, always two steps ahead. But that was before everything fell apart. Before he was discharged. Before the financial ruin that followed. Ethan's bitterness had festered, turning him into someone who couldn't stop ruminating. He now saw enemies everywhere, even in former friends. Jared knew this wasn't a spur-of-the-moment decision. Ethan had planned every detail, just like he used to, but now with a vengeful heart.

The pond lay between them, its surface marred by swirling oil and toxic waste. Beneath the water, a distorted figure was settled. The ripples seemed to mock Jared. They taunted him with a future Ethan had designed. His best friend John had been lured here and trapped, just like Jared was now. The same fate that had claimed John was planned for Jared. He could feel it in his bones.

He looked over at Jillian, clutching the stack of papers that held the key to exposing Ethan's crimes. Her hands couldn't hold the documents any tighter. Her eyes met Jared's, filled with a silent plea, a desperate hope that somehow, they would make it out alive.

But Ethan wasn't going to let that happen. He had spent years poisoning the pond, dumping toxic waste without a second thought. And now, with plans already in motion at the morgue, he was ready to finish what he started.

As Ethan prepared to aim, Jared instinctively moved in front of Jillian, shielding her with his body. He was a soldier, and he would protect Jillian with everything he had. The cold look in Ethan's eyes wasn't new. But it was darker now, more dangerous. This wasn't just about money. It was about revenge. Ethan blamed everyone who didn't stand with him as his enemy. In his eyes, he knew they couldn't be trusted. Jared knew, words wouldn't be enough to stop him.

Ethan's voice was low and venomous. "You stood by and watched, Jared. You let them destroy me. You're no better than the rest of them."

Jared met his gaze, seeing the pain and anger that had twisted Ethan's mind. "You think killing us will help you? That it'll give you a chance?"

"It's not about making things right," Ethan hissed. "It's about making sure it never happens again. Evil needs to be purged, and you're part of that rot."

The hammer of the gun clicked back with a slow, deliberate motion, the sound echoing in the still air.

Cla-Click.

Jared's heart raced. He locked eyes with Jillian, silently promising her that he wasn't going down without a fight. He saw the fear in her eyes, but also something else—trust. She believed in him, believed that he could save them.

Ethan's breath came out in shallow puffs, visible in the cold air. Jared braced himself, every muscle in his body tense. This was it.

Bang! Bang! Bang!

The gunshots shattered the silence, each one louder and more final than the last. Jared flinched, his entire body tensing for the impact. He squeezed his eyes shut, waiting for the searing pain to tear through him. But it never came.

Slowly, he opened his eyes. The water in the pond was churning, boiling like something alive. Ethan's triumphant grin had vanished, replaced by a look of pure rage. From the depths of the pond, a gnarled, gray hand emerged, clawing its way up from the mud. Bullets tore through its flesh, but the creature didn't stop. It kept coming, relentless and unstoppable.

Jared's heart pounded in his chest. The ripples on the pond's surface revealed a terrible truth. It wasn't just poisoned—it was alive with something dark. Ethan's greed had awakened it.

The creature's grip tightened around Ethan's ankle, dragging him toward the water with ruthless strength.

"Get to the car!" Jared's voice was hoarse, filled with urgency. He grabbed Jillian's hand, pulling her away from the water's edge. He had already lost John—he wasn't about to lose her too. Jillian stumbled, her mind reeling from the shock. Behind them, the revolver clicked empty as Ethan struggled in vain against the force dragging him down.

Ethan's screams filled the air, a sound of pure terror that made Jared's blood run cold. But there was nothing he could do. Ethan had made his choices, and now he was paying the price.

Jared didn't look back. He couldn't. He had to keep moving, had to get Jillian to safety. The lesson was clear: evil always comes back around.

As they sped away, the forest closed in. The trees cast jagged, shifting patterns across the road. But Jared couldn't shake the feeling that this was only the beginning. The pond might have claimed Ethan, but it wasn't done. Not yet.

In the rearview mirror, the pond came into view one last time, now eerily still. For a moment, Jared thought he saw something. Two cold, calculating eyes stared back at him from beneath the water. Eyes that reminded him of Ethan.

But before he could be sure, the car sped around the bend, and the pond was gone, swallowed by the trees.

REMAIN UNSEEN

ETHAN CURSED under his breath as Jared and Jillian's car disappeared into the distance. "Figures," he muttered, kicking away the skeletal hand that had latched onto his levAVg. The creature's grip had loosened. Its lifeless fingers crumbled into the mud after Ethan's relentless assault. They had gotten away — again. *Always them. Always meddling, always getting in the way.*

As the stillness returned to the pond, Ethan's eyes lingered on the water, now calm but unnervingly reflective. That gray, clawing hand haunted him. It reminded him that his problems were growing more complicated by the day. Scanning the horizon, he ensured no one else had witnessed the horror that had just unfolded. It was time to cover his tracks. Jared and

Jillian had slipped through his fingers, but he knew they'd cross paths again. They always did. And if not, well, he'd make sure to find them first.

Reaching behind the seat of his truck, Ethan pulled out a roll of black plastic. *Money. It all comes down to money.* The thought repeated in his mind like a mantra as he tugged on his gloves. His grip slipped slightly under the weight of the wrapped figure. *Ever since I lost my job, it's been a struggle. Then Liz...* His late wife's name flickered through his mind, but he shoved the memory away. *Control. I need control. Without money, there's no control. And without control, I'm just another nobody.*

As he worked, a harsh caw echoed through the trees, making him pause. Ethan glanced up. A group of ravens perched on the branches above, their black feathers ruffled by the wind. Their eyes seemed to bore into him, unblinking and unnerving. He scowled and shook his head, trying to dismiss the unease that prickled at his skin.

"Just birds," he muttered, though their presence lingered in the back of his mind. The ravens cawed again. Their sound grated on his nerves. He continued dragging the wrapped figure out of the mud and up from the pond's edge.

The woods around him were dense and silent, save for the occasional rustling of leaves. The trees loomed tall. Their branches twisted and swayed, as if alive with some unseen force. Ethan eyed a large tree. Its gnarled, exposed roots snaked out of the ground like the tentacles of some ancient beast. The wind picked up, causing the branches to creak and groan ominously. For a brief moment, the thought of the tree toppling over flashed through his mind, but he shook it off with a grunt.

"Never again," he muttered, his frustration simmering beneath the surface. "I wouldn't be in this mess if it weren't for them." He grunted with effort, finally hoisting the remains behind the seat, inside the of truck. His movements were precise and methodical. They were just another task in a long line of tasks he was too used to. Covering his tracks had become second nature. It didn't matter who—or what—was beneath the plastic. It had to go.

The truck's engine roared to life as Ethan sped down the back roads, his thoughts racing even faster. *Money buys freedom. Money buys power. Without it, I'm just another sucker working a dead-end job. But with it, I can make things happen. Change things. He tightened his grip on the steering wheel. The weight of his actions pressed on him like a suffocating blanket.*

Ahead, the funeral home loomed. Its faded sign creaked in the breeze: "Town of Elmhurst Funeral Home.""

The air was thick with the smell of chemicals and decay. Ethan stepped inside. The metal gurney, a wheeled stretcher for bodies, was ready as planned. His hands moved quickly, out of habit. The only feeling he had left was relief. He rolled the body into the incineration room, where the furnace had cooled. *This is what it takes. This is what keeps me ahead,* he thought. *First the man at the Gas station, then John.*

They won't stay gone. He angrily pushed the wrapped body into the retort — a fitting name for the furnace since it had the final say. After closing the door, he knew the EPA would be furious about burning plastic, but they wouldn't be coming back.

"Come test for that!" He mocked the burning door.

As the body began to burn, the door swung open with a creak. Victor, the owner, strolled in, a knowing smile playing on his lips. "Another one bites the dust, huh?" He lit a cigarette with casual ease, his eyes never leaving Ethan's face.

Ethan coughed as the smoke hit his throat. "I'm here for your pick-up."

Victor nodded, handing him a thick envelope. "Here's your money. Those environmental nuts have been sniffing around again. John from the EPA was here last week, asking too many questions. I figured it was you who fired up the furnace."

Ethan opened the door, revealing the fire inside. Their gazes flicked to the flames as they consumed the last remnants of evidence. "Yeah, I dealt with him for you. I'm still cleaning up that mess." He closed the door, and it boomed shut, a final sense of completion settling over the room.

Victor smirked, taking a long drag from his cigarette. "I trust you'll handle it. Election's this week, and once I'm on the town council, we'll have the freedom to move funds around as needed. We'll get those drain lines set up for waste disposal, no problem. And of course, I'll keep you paid. These chemicals from the morgue? Safe as houses once they're diluted. But you know how people are—there's always some idiot who thinks we're mutating the wildlife." He scoffed, shaking his head. "Thanks for taking care of John and everyone else in my way. I'm running unopposed now, thanks to you. You'll be making more money once we're fully operational."

Ethan pocketed the envelope, the weight of it reassuring. *Secure. Powerful. Untouchable. At least Victor gets it.* He moved to the tanker truck, hooking up a hose to siphon the fluid from the morgue's storage tanks. Soon, all of this would go into the public water system. It would eliminate the need for these night runs. As the last of the fluid drained into the tanker, he disconnected the hose, careful not to spill a drop. By the time the furnace had consumed everything, he was back in the truck, driving away from the funeral home.

The drive to the secluded woods was long and silent. Only the ticking of the cooling engine kept him company. Ethan's mind wandered, tracing the strange path that had led him here. *Jobless. Penniless. Left with nothing after Liz died. Now, I have control. I have power. And no one's going to take that from me.* He reached the secluded spot by the river, the only sound the distant rush of water over rocks.

As he stepped out into the night, the cold air biting against his skin, he noticed the ravens again. They were in the trees, their dark forms barely visible against the night sky. But, their presence was unmistakable. Ethan frowned, trying to ignore the uneasy feeling that had settled in his gut.

He opened the tanker valve. The chemical waste poured out, a thick, noxious stream that vanished into the river. A foul odor filled the air, carried away by the breeze. *If those idiots at the EPA weren't so nosy, I wouldn't have to drive this far.* He watched the liquid dissolve into the water, the current carrying it away.

But the trees around him creaked and swayed. The wind rustled through their branches like whispered warnings. The ravens' caws echoed in the darkness, their cries harsh and relentless. Ethan's eyes darted around the forest, his heart pounding faster as the feeling of being watched intensified.

His thoughts drifted back to Jared and Jillian. They were out there, hunting for proof. He needed to discredit them before they could cause any real trouble. *The next time I see them, I won't miss.* He slipped his gun into his pocket, his resolve hardening as he climbed back into the truck.

But as he drove away, the eerie calls of the ravens followed him, mingling with the creaking of the trees. The darkness felt alive, with whispers of unseen threats floating on the breeze. The air was sharp against his skin as he cracked the window, letting the cold night invade the cab.

Despite his best efforts, Ethan felt something watching him from the shadows. The night was hiding it. And for the first time in a long while, Ethan felt truly afraid.

FLOWING THROUGH THE TREES

A PUNGENT CHEMICAL stench seeped into the car as Jared and Jillian drove down the winding road. Their escape was still fresh in their minds. They quickly rolled up the windows. It blocked the noxious air but not the memory of Ethan being dragged into the pond. The image of that gray, skeletal hand clinging to him was burned into their consciousness. Neither of them knew if he had survived, but the thought alone was enough to keep their nerves on edge.

"What was that thing?" Jillian gasped, her voice trembling as she clutched the seat. The horror of the creature's hand—its cold, gray skin—haunted her. She shuddered involuntarily.

Jared glanced at her, his own thoughts racing. His hand trembled slightly on the steering wheel, a tremor he quickly stilled. "You're the biologist. Any theories?" he inquired, though he already knew no textbook had prepared her for what they'd seen. "My friend Allen's place is just a couple of miles up the road. We need to get there. He might have some answers."

"Do you think he knows what's happening?"

Jared exhaled deeply, the weight of their situation pressing down on him. "If anyone does, it's Allen. He's been through a lot—he might know something we don't."

The narrow gravel road wound through the dense forest. Each bump in the road seemed to magnify their tension. It felt as if those who didn't run fast enough, were buried beneath the rocks. The cabin came into view at last. It was a small, isolated structure, nestled among the trees. It was a peaceful setting despite it all.

Jared's heart tightened as memories of John flashed through his mind—John, who was gone because of Ethan. Allen was still recovering from a near-fatal accident. Now, Jared had to break the news about John.

"Allen!" Jared called out as they reached the porch, his voice echoing in the stillness. The door creaked open slowly, revealing Allen's pale, gaunt face. His eyes, once sharp and full of life, now flickered nervously between Jared and Jillian.

"Get in, quickly!" Allen urged, his voice strained as he hobbled back to let them inside. He moved slowly, every step a painful reminder of the accident that had left him broken.

They stepped into the dim cabin. The air was thick with the stale scent of coffee and something metallic. It was cold and unsettling. Allen, using his crutches, bolted the door with a swift, practiced motion. Jillian first saw a man who had once been strong, a protector. Now, he seemed vulnerable and exposed. The cabin, like Allen himself, seemed worn down by the weight of too many battles.

"Look," Allen whispered, his voice low as he gestured for them to sit. "I don't know how much time we have."

"Allen, listen—" Jared started, but Allen cut him off with a sharp wave of his hand.

"There's no time," Allen muttered, his voice barely audible over the sound of their own breathing. His words carried the weight of a man who had seen too much, who had lost too much. The confidence Jared once knew was now buried beneath layers of pain and fear.

Jillian looked at Jared, her eyes full of unspoken questions. She searched for something—anything—that made sense.

Allen's face tightened, his eyes narrowing. "You saw it, didn't you? I can see it in your eyes." Allen was looking for answers of his own.

Jillian shivered as the memory of the creature's unnatural form resurfaced. Before she could respond, a low growl rumbled through the cabin. Then, she heard the unmistakable scrape of nails on wood. She could feel the sound on her skin, freezing her in place.

Allen's hand shot out, grabbing the shotgun that leaned against the wall. Despite his injuries, his movements were quick and precise, driven by a soldier's instinct to protect. The front door rattled violently, the hinges groaning under the pressure. Allen raised the shotgun, his jaw set with grim determination. "Get ready," he mouthed to Jared and Jillian.

A heavy thud resonated from outside, the noise sending a jolt of adrenaline through them. Allen's eyes flicked to the window, scanning the darkness beyond. "I saw something running across the field a few weeks ago," he confirmed, his voice tight. "It was carrying a wet wrench. I've been seeing things ever since."

Jared's mind flashed back to their military days. Allen had always been the first to spot danger, the first to act. Even now, injured and weary, he hadn't lost that edge. The three of them stood together, tense. They listened to the rumbling outside, then a thunderous boom shook the trees.

A growl, not of this world, erupted from the treeline. It reverberated through the cabin, shaking the walls and rattling the windows. Allen tightened his grip on the shotgun. "Stay close," he ordered, limping toward the back door. Jared and Jillian followed, their breaths coming in short, rapid gasps.

Allen creaked the door open with his gun. In the distance, a large, twisted shadow loomed near the edge of the trees, its form barely visible in the dim light. The shape thrashed violently, just out of view. It was as if some monstrous thing was trying to break free from the night.

Jared swallowed hard, his pulse racing. Whatever was out there, it wasn't going to stop until it got what it wanted.

Allen's eyes darted around, searching the trees for movement. Jared felt a tremor run through his hand again. He tried to ignore it, focusing on the immediate danger, but the tremor wouldn't go away.

Jillian grabbed Jared's arm, her grip tight. "What is it?" she whispered, her voice barely audible over the pounding of their hearts.

Allen didn't answer immediately, his gaze fixed on the trees. "It's not just one thing," he murmured finally, his voice grim.

BEASTS

ALLEN STEPPED FORWARD. Each movement made him grit his teeth, pushing past the pain of his injuries. He was using one crutch, which creaked under the weight of his body. The shotgun in his other hand led the way, an extension of his resolve. Behind him, Jared and Jillian moved cautiously. Their eyes studied the trees. Every shadow was a potential threat.

"Stay behind me, and keep quiet," Allen whispered, his voice strained yet commanding. The cabin's interior was thick with the smell of pine. It mixed with the damp, earthy scent that clung to everything in the forest.

The dim light from outside cast restless shadows that seemed to writhe with intent. The air was thick, fouled by a stench that drew swarms of flies, buzzing and gathering around the cabin. Then, without warning, a creature bolted from the woods, a blur of motion and malice.

BANG! BANG!

Allen didn't hesitate. The creature howled, then crashed through the underbrush. The trees trembled as something much larger stirred on the other side of the field, concealed in the shade of the canopy.

"What the hell was that?!" Jared called out, his voice tight with anxiety. His eyes spotting the tree line, every movement magnifying the tension coiled inside him.

"Let's move, soldier," Allen shouted. He pushed forward, his crutch digging into the dew-drenched grass. "I'm trying to scare the others off." Their footsteps sank into the soft peat moss, turning the lush green into a dark, muddy trail. The grass tore open beneath them, leaving behind a wake of churned earth as they crossed the clearing. In the distance, thunder rumbled, another storm was on the horizon.

As they approached the tree line, a rustling sound broke the uneasy silence. Allen froze, raising a hand to signal the others to stop.

"What am I hearing?" Jillian whispered. The forest around them seemed to close in, the trees looming overhead, their branches swaying eerily in the wind.

Then Jillian gasped, her hands flying to her mouth in shock. The papers she had been clutching slipped from her grasp. They scattered across the clearing like distressed birds caught in a sudden gust of wind.

"What... what is that?" her voice barely audible over the pounding of her heart. She stared at the thing before them—a grotesque blend of nightmare and reality.

In the dim space between two large oaks stood a sturdy, bent, and scarred metal cage. It appeared as if a creature had broken out before, but wouldn't again. The beast within was barely visible in the gloom, a dark mass that jerked and thrashed in silence. Its maw opened and closed in a grotesque imitation of life. It revealed rotting, decaying teeth. A noxious chemical stench seeped from its mouth. It was a sickly sweet odor that clung to the air, making it almost unbearable to breathe. Its unnervingly large, fixed eyes bore into Jillian, cold and motionless. The stare radiated a chilling intensity, compelling her to run.

Jillian took a step back, her entire body shuddering under the weight of the creature's gaze. The creature's presence was born from a toxic nightmare. The result of a corruption that had seeped into the land.

The creature didn't move. It was focused on Jillian. Allen knelt by the trap, horrified and fascinated as he examined it.

"This is what the poison does," Allen asserted, his voice steady despite the fear gnawing at his insides. "This is what's out there, what's happening to the wildlife when they drink the polluted waters. I've got trail cameras set up around the property, but no one would believe the footage. This, though... this thing is still alive."

Jillian's eyes widened in disbelief. "Cameras? What else have you seen?"

Allen nodded grimly. "Enough to know this is just the beginning." He paused, studying the creature's matted fur, the patches of exposed, blistered skin. "There's more footage out there, some from cameras I haven't even checked recently. But the people need to see the real deal. This isn't fake — it's breathing, it's alive, and it's changing."

"Is this... a dog?" Jillian murmured, glancing nervously around the clearing. The forest seemed to close in on them, the air growing heavier, more suffocating. The trees groaned in the wind, casting long, distorted forms that flickered on the ground like restless spirits.

Allen looked at Jillian and Jared, the fear in their eyes mirroring his own. "Running away won't solve this. There's something in the water, something that's warping everything it touches. The wildlife, the land — it's all changing."

He turned his gaze back to the creature, seeing it fully for the first time. Its form was grotesque, oversized, and deformed. Yet, it was hauntingly familiar.

"Look at it," Allen insisted, his voice filled with a quiet determination. "The real question is... is it getting worse?"

The creature in the cage was a twisted remnant of a dog. It was a living testament to the corruption they were fighting. Its body was warped and unnatural, a demon of the strays Jared used to chase away from the pond. But now, it was something else entirely — something far more sinister.

"We'll figure it out," Jillian confirmed, though her voice was laced with uncertainty. It was as much a reassurance to herself as it was to anyone else.

Allen gave her a resolute nod. "Together, we'll fix this. But we need to get inside, now. There's more of them out there—I've seen tracks, heard noises at night, animals disappearing. At first, I thought it was just my mind. Then, I saw one of these things dragging a man across the field. I came out here and found a wrench— it's the one I gave you, Jared. If I hadn't caught this one, everyone would think I was losing it."

He paused, his eyes distant, lost in thought. "So, I started setting traps, trying to make sure I wasn't just seeing things. I needed answers, but now…" He trailed off, his voice heavy with uncertainty. "Now I don't even know what to do."

Jillian quickly gathered her scattered papers, her hands trembling as she struggled to keep her composure. "This wasn't what I was expecting."

The creature in the cage remained still, its breathing shallow, its eyes locked onto Jillian. It was as if it recognized her, as if it knew she was part of the threat it now faced.

"Do you think there are more out there?"

Allen nodded grimly, his expression grave. "I'm sure of it." Suddenly, a low growl rumbled through the air. From the corner of his eye, Allen saw something approaching in the distance.

They were not alone.

STORM CLOUDS

ALLEN GLANCED back at the cage one last time, the creature within still watching them. It was breathing but also was forcing itself to remember.

"Let's move," he directed, his voice low and urgent. There was no time for hesitation. "We need to get inside."

The trio hurried across the field, the wet leaves and twigs crunching beneath their feet. Each step filled with the weight of impending danger. The distant rumble of thunder reverberated through the air, adding a sense of urgency to their movements. Allen's mind raced—had the gunshots drawn unwanted attention? He could feel the storm gathering above. Dark clouds swirled, heavy with the promise of rain.

Suddenly, a rustling sound broke the tense silence. Allen's eyes snapped to the tree line, his finger instinctively hovering over the trigger of his shotgun.

"Did you hear that?" Jared paused, his voice betraying the fear that had settled in the pit of his stomach.

Allen's gaze swept the trees, his senses on high alert, every nerve tingling with anticipation. And then he saw them. Something moved along the ground, slinking through the underbrush.

"Get inside now!" Allen barked, his voice sharp and commanding. It cut through the thick air and the rising screeches echoing from the trees.

The creature in the cage snapped its jaws at the air, its nostrils flaring as it caught the scent of something on the wind. Allen began limping back toward the cabin, his crutch sinking into the wet mud as thunder rolled in overhead. The sky darkened, as if a giant hand was closing into a fist. The weight of doom pressed down on them from all sides. Fat raindrops began to fall, smacking against the leaves and drenching the earth. Whatever was out there seemed to melt back into the wilderness, retreating from the rain.

Inside the house, Allen bolted the door, collapsing against it as he struggled to catch his breath. The pounding rain on the roof echoed the frantic beat of his heart, a constant reminder of the danger lurking just outside.

"What the hell was that noise?" Jared gasped, his eyes wide, searching the room without truly seeing anything.

"I don't know," Allen replied, his voice grim, laced with the uncertainty he rarely allowed himself to feel. "It's something watching us from the tree line."

Jillian's hands shook as she pulled out her phone. "I'm calling animal control. They need to come get that dog before its smell attracts whatever is out there."

Allen nodded, though his thoughts were far from settled. As Jillian made the call, Allen raised his own phone, snapping photos of the cage through the rain-streaked window. He noted every detail, every sign of trouble. His instincts told him that they would need this evidence—sooner rather than later. The rain poured outside, a relentless torrent. It deepened the eerie atmosphere. The cabin felt less safe and more a fragile refuge.

As Allen stared out the window, something caught his eye—movement in the trees. The shadows weren't just the night playing tricks on them. He could see beady eyes glinting as they studied the cabin. On the ground, the underbrush rustled as something prowled, their low growls barely audible over the sound of the rain.

It wasn't long before the animal control truck arrived, headlights cutting through the murky twilight. Allen met the officers at the door, his expression serious.

"The dog is in the cage out back," his voice steady but filled with an undercurrent of tension. "But be careful. There's something out there in the woods—something is circling us."

The officers exchanged smirks then nodded. They moved quickly across the field, rain soaking them to the bone. They approached the cage. The storm lashed at them. The rain blurred their vision. The trees closed in around them, a wall of dark, twisted branches.

The officers scanned the tree line, something felt off. Allen raised his phone, snapping photos of what was unfolding. The real danger wasn't behind bars. Then, in the distance, something shifted. A creature, barely visible, watched them. It had the same gaze as the one in the cage.

One officer hesitated, his finger hovering over trigger of his tranquilizer gun. The rain continued to fall, the storm's fury growing. Whatever else was out there was closing in...

FACING THE STORM

ALLEN WATCHED from the porch, his eyes sharp, his shotgun resting within easy reach. The rain had slowed to a steady drizzle, turning the ground into a slick, muddy mess. The animal control officers worked swiftly. They tranquilized the mutated dog, then carefully loaded it into their truck. Allen snapped more photos, his phone capturing every detail, every sign that something was horribly wrong in their town.

One of the officers approached, his expression a mixture of curiosity and concern. "Can I ask you all a couple of questions? We're sending this one to a lab, see if we can figure out what this creature really is."

Jillian stepped forward, shuffling through her paperwork with a determined look on her face. "Here," she said, offering a document with a slight smile, "this report from Salvo might help."

The officer took the report, flipping through the pages, his brow furrowing as he scanned the information. "What's this?" he asked, his voice heavy with the weight of the implications.

"I'm Dr. Simons. I'm a biologist from the coast," Jillian explained. "That report shows mutations appearing in the coastal area. I believe what's happening here is connected."

The officer looked up, concern etched into his features. "You might want to bring this up at the town meeting tomorrow. This is the kind of thing everyone needs to hear."

"Meeting?" Jillian asked, taken aback.

"Yes, ma'am," the officer continued. "There's a town meeting scheduled for tomorrow. With the council elections coming up, everyone's gathering to discuss a few things. It might be a good time to bring this to light."

Jillian nodded, absorbing the information. "Thank you. We'll be there."

With the immediate threat temporarily subdued, Allen turned to Jillian and Jared. His mind had shifted to the next challenge, despite the situation's importance.

"We need to be at that meeting tomorrow. It's our chance to confront what's happening head-on, to get some answers and make sure people understand the danger."

Jillian glanced around the room, taking in the boarded-up windows, the makeshift barricades. "It looks like you've already started preparing," she observed, her tone laced with concern.

"Only the paranoid and prepared survive," Allen replied, his voice low, almost resigned. Something he lived by.

"Come on now," Jared interjected, trying to lighten the mood. "The ones behind all this—they're tearing the world apart, even if they don't realize it. That's why Jillian is here. She grew up watching pollution affect the sea turtles. The world needs more people like her, who know what they're talking about. We need people who care enough to make a difference."

"Things are changing in this little town," Allen sighed, his gaze distant. "Jillian's evidence could be what we need to bring an end to this... whatever it is that's happening out there."

Jared leaned in, his voice dropping to a more serious tone. "We need to reset the trap. Ethan destroyed all the hard evidence we had against him. The only thing I can think of is to catch him in the act again. But what we really need is to push for real regulations—something that can prevent this kind of thing from even being possible. Disposal companies need to report directly to regulators, not just pay fines and go back to business as usual."

Allen leaned back in his chair, staring out the window, lost in thought. "That's a good point, Jared. But around here, people only know me from my store—the Military Surplus Store downtown. I'm not sure how much good I'll be in changing anything."

"Allen, everyone is essential," Jared insisted. "Your store has been a cornerstone in this town for generations. People trust you."

The next morning, the storm had passed, leaving the town drenched but calm, the air thick with the smell of wet earth and lingering tension. Allen stood in front of the mirror, adjusting his tie. It had been a long time since he'd dressed up for anything, but today was important. Today, he wasn't just Allen Boyd, the man who had barely survived an accident—he was someone who might help save his town.

"Ready?" Jillian asked, appearing in the doorway. She looked composed, her determination a stark contrast to the fear she had felt the night before.

Allen nodded, giving her a faint smile. "A suit and crutches—I'm quite the sight. But today, we're making a stand. I've got a surprise for everyone."

The town hall was buzzing with activity when they arrived. People gathered in small groups, their conversations hushed, filled with speculation and rumor. The air was thick with the unspoken secrets of the town, the weight of the past few days pressing down on everyone. As they entered, Allen was greeted by Victor, who was running for his position on the town council. Victor's smile was wide, too wide, as he worked the crowd with the practiced ease of a seasoned politician.

As they mingled, they overheard Victor speaking to a group of local business owners, his tone conspiratorial. "Listen," Victor began, his voice low but carrying, "we all know this town needs better handling of waste. My trucks can only do so much, but I've just broken ground on a new treatment center that's going to help clean this town up."

One of the business owners, a portly man with a red face, nodded eagerly. "Tell us more, Victor. We've been wondering if your company was going to step up and help out. We know it's helped your businesses a lot."

Victor smiled, a predatory gleam in his eyes. "That's exactly why I'm running. I want to get this town cleaned up, no more sludge-filled trucks crossing state lines. I handle my company, but I also want to make our town better. We both live here, after all."

Allen listened, a knot of anxiety tightening in his stomach. Victor's words dripped with false promises, the kind that had led to the very situation they were in now.

The mayor, an older man with a stern expression, stepped up to the podium, tapping the microphone to get the crowd's attention.

"Ladies and gentlemen," the mayor began, his voice clear. "We have important announcements today about the town council. Unfortunately, due to unforeseen circumstances, another candidate has dropped out. This leaves Victor unopposed... or at least, it would have."

The crowd murmured, curiosity buzzing through the room like static electricity. Allen felt a surge of nerves, his heart pounding in his chest.

"I want everyone to please welcome Allen Boyd," the mayor continued, his voice ringing out. "Owner of the Military Surplus Store and long-time resident of our town. Your new candidate running for the town council."

The room erupted into applause, the sound a mix of surprise and support. Victor's smile faltered, his eyes narrowing as he glared up at the podium. Allen was now his opponent—something Victor needed dealt with.

AT THE PODIUM

ALLEN'S ENTERENCE silenced the room. They now saw the familiar man from the Military Surplus Store in a different light. He was vulnerable, yet unwavering. His crutches made soft thuds on the wooden floor as he approached the podium, each step a testament to his resolve. The town didn't expect this. A man they saw as steady and reliable now showed both his strength and his heart.

Clearing his throat, Allen looked at the sea of faces. Their expressions ranged from curious to skeptical. The weight of the moment pressed down on him, but he drew strength from the supportive gazes of Jared and Jillian seated in the front row.

"Good evening, everyone," Allen began, his voice steady as it flowed through the silent hall. "My name is

Allen Boyd, and most of you know me from my store. But today, I'm here not just as a business owner, but as someone who cares deeply about our community—about the future of this town."

He paused, letting his words sink in. His eyes met Victor's cold, calculating gaze, and a subtle tension rippled through the room. "We've all heard about the issues plaguing our town—the toxic pond, the illegal waste dumping that's been going on right under our noses. And we've all felt the impact, whether we realize it or not. I've seen it firsthand, and I know many of you have too."

A murmur spread through the crowd, a mix of agreement and concern. Some nodded, sharing knowing glances, while others whispered anxiously among themselves. Allen took a deep breath, drawing courage from the murmurs of support that grew louder with each passing second.

"Next time you see me, I'll be off these crutches," Allen continued, a note of determination in his voice. "But what this town needs is more than just physical recovery—it needs a big change. That's why I'm running for the town council. I've decided to sell my store to focus entirely on cleaning up our community, for everyone's sake. We need real change—not just someone who's going to use the town for their own profit. We need to protect our environment, our health, and our future. It's not until you lose your health that you realize how important it is. And it's not until your town is at risk that you realize how much you need to fight for it."

The murmurs turned into a buzz of rising hope and agreement. Victor's confident smile faded, replaced by a mask of concern as he realized the tide was turning against him.

"Together," Allen's voice grew stronger, filling the room with a sense of purpose, "we can make our town better for everyone—not just for a select few. I promise to fight for you, for our children, and for the future of our community. Thank you."

The applause was overwhelming, a wave of support that filled the hall. Allen stepped back from the podium, a surge of relief washing over him. He had taken the first step in what he knew would be a long and challenging battle, but he felt a renewed sense of purpose. With Jared and Jillian by his side, he was ready to face whatever came next.

As they made their way outside, a small black car spun it's tires out in the parking lot. The cool evening air wrapped around them, a stark contrast to the heated tension inside the town hall. The sounds of the people faded into the distance, replaced by the quiet murmurs of the night. As they neared their car, a shadow broke from the building. It was Victor, slipping into the darkness, his face twisted with fury.

Victor pulled out his phone, his hands shaking with barely restrained anger. He dialed Ethan's number, his voice trembling as he spat out his frustration. "Ethan! Where are you?"

Ethan's voice crackled through the speaker, cold and detached. "I'm not far from town. What's the problem?"

"Allen! Allen Boyd!" Victor seethed, his breath coming in short, angry bursts. "He's running for the council, and he's stirring up trouble about the waste dumping. We need to deal with him before he ruins everything!"

"I've already taken care of the other candidates and John," Ethan replied, his tone chilling in its calmness. "We'll handle Allen too. Just keep an eye on him and let me know where he's going to be."

Victor ended the call, his mind churning with thoughts of revenge. He slammed his fist into the brick wall. The rough surface scraped his knuckles, sending a sharp sting through his hand. The unyielding bricks seemed to mock him, a reminder of the obstacles closing in from all sides. Allen Boyd wasn't supposed to become a problem. Yet here he was, threatening everything Victor had worked so hard to control.

Victor leaned against the wall, the night's chill creeping through his jacket as he tried to steady his racing mind. He felt the familiar weight of his revolver in his pocket. Perfect. Pulling it free, he stayed hidden in the shadows, his eyes scanning the street as if searching for them. Then his heart skipped a beat. The car—it was gone. The one Jillian, Jared, and Allen had taken. He'd been so lost in his fury, he hadn't even noticed which way they went.

A creeping sense of dread clawed at him as the pieces fell into place. They weren't just running errands. They were making a move—a move against him.

Victor's breath slowed, a wicked smile curling his lips. They thought they could outrun him. Outmaneuver him?

They had no idea what was coming.

As the shadows swallowed him, dark thoughts raced through his mind, already plotting the next step. One way or another, Allen Boyd wouldn't make it to that town hall meeting.

Not alive.

IN THE SHADOWS

THE APPLAUSE from the town hall still rang in Allen's ears as they left. But, the cheers were quickly replaced by the weight of what lay ahead. The responsibility they had just shouldered settled heavily on their minds.

The car ride was silent at first, the tension present as Jillian navigated the dark roads. Allen finally broke the silence, his voice low and serious. "We can't waste any time. Let's stop by my Military Surplus store. I have a few ideas… like getting some trail cameras set up around Victor's place."

"Allen!" Jared interrupted suddenly, his tone sharp.

Allen flinched, caught off guard. "What? There was something about the way Victor mentioned disposing of those chemicals that didn't sit right with me."

Jared's eyes widened as the pieces clicked together. "Your cameras—some of them are still at my place. John's disappearance, everything that's happened... it might all be on those cameras."

The realization hit them both. The cameras around the pond, still active, might hold the key to exposing Ethan and Victor once and for all. As the car sped through the darkening countryside, Jared and Jillian filled Allen in on the events that had transpired. They recounted their harrowing encounter with Ethan, and the creature that had emerged from the depths of the pond.

The night crept in, swallowing the light as they drove past the pond. Ethan's truck was gone, leaving the area eerily silent.

Allen noticed Jared's hands trembling, the knuckles white as he gripped his seat. Concern flickered across Allen's face, but he kept his voice steady. "Jared, are you okay? Your hands... they're shaking."

Jared quickly withdrew his hands, clenching them into tight fists. "It's nothing," he muttered, his voice strained as he turned away. "I'll go get the cameras."

Allen, sensing that something was off, nodded but wasn't fully convinced. "Jillian, keep the car running," he instructed, his tone more urgent. He glanced around the darkened landscape, every shadow seeming to hide a lurking threat.

As they stepped out of the car, the air was thick with the scent of damp earth and decaying leaves. Allen kept a vigilant watch, his eyes scanning the tree line for any sign of movement. Jillian's gaze drifted toward the pond, the water's surface barely visible in the fading light. Her breath caught as she noticed something—a faint glint, as if something was moving just beneath the water.

Unsure of what she had seen, Jillian kept her eyes locked on the water's edge, every muscle in her body tense.

Jared made his way to the first trail camera, crouching low as he reached it. He cursed under his breath when he realized it wasn't running. "Damn it... I hope the others caught something," he muttered to himself before cutting across to the second camera.

As Jared moved deeper into the woods, the night seemed to close in around him. The trees rustled with an unsettling sound, and the forest seemed to come alive with whispers of danger. The second camera was still operational, its blinking light a small beacon in the dark. Jared quickly retrieved it. His pulse quickened as strange, familiar smells wafted through the trees. They were dark, chemical scents that brought back memories of the pond. Memories of the creatures breath.

Jared hurried to the final camera, but the unsettling noises in the forest grew louder, more pronounced. Something was coming, something large and dangerous.

Jillian's breath hitched as she watched from the car, her eyes wide with fear. "What was that?" she whispered, her voice trembling.

Jared turned towards the car, his heart pounding in his chest. He could see the fear in Jillian's eyes, her face pale in the dim light. He didn't need to hear the sounds to know something was wrong—he could feel it in the air, a sense of impending dread.

"Get in, now!" Allen's voice cut through the night, urgent and commanding as he threw open the car door.

Jared sprinted towards the car, clutching the cameras tightly. The forest behind him seemed to come alive, the snapping of branches and guttural growls growing closer, louder.

Just as Jared dove into the car, the headlights lit something large at the forest's edge. A shadowy figure, hulking and monstrous, sent a wave of terror through Jillian.

Allen slammed the door shut, the noise echoing in the confined space of the car. But the relief was short-lived as the sounds outside grew more frenzied. The unmistakable sound of something being dragged across the ground reached their ears. The sound of fabric being ripped apart.

"What's that noise?!" Jared's voice was frantic as he looked around, his eyes darting to the backseat. But his breath caught in his throat when he realized—"Where's Allen?"

CAUGHT IN THE NIGHT

"ALLEN!" Jared's voice rang out, laced with panic as he watched his friend being dragged away into the darkness. His heart pounded in his chest, and without thinking, he dropped the cameras and lunged for the door handle, ready to throw himself into the night. But Jillian's hand shot out, grabbing his arm in a firm grip.

"Wait! We need to be smart about this," she urged, her own fear barely contained as she tried to keep her voice steady. "What if more of those things are out there?"

The grinding sound of rocks scraping against each other revealed enough. Allen was being pulled farther from the safety of the car. Jared didn't hesitate.

"I can't just leave him out there," Jared growled, shaking off Jillian's grip.

Without another word, he flung the car door open and sprinted toward the shadowy figure dragging Allen away. Jillian watched, her heart in her throat as the scene unfolded before her.

The creature, its massive jaws clamped around Allen's shoe, was pulling him relentlessly across the ground. Jared, fueled by adrenaline spotted one of Allen's crutches lying on the ground. Grabbing it, he swung with all his might, the crutch connecting with a sickening thud against the creature's nose.

"Get off him!" Jared shouted, his voice raw with fear and anger as he prepared to swing again. The drooling beast released Allen with a snarl, turning its malevolent gaze toward Jared, who stood his ground.

"Get in the car!" Jared yelled, not taking his eyes off the creature. Allen, gasping in pain, managed to stagger to his feet and shuffle toward the car. Jared listened intently, straining to hear any movement from the surrounding trees. He knew that more could be lurking in the shadows.

With every ounce of strength he had left, Allen crawled into the back seat as Jillian revved the engine, her focus on Jared. The creature began circling the car, its eyes still locked on Allen, its movements slow and deliberate, as if it was savoring the hunt.

Jared, still gripping the crutch, climbed into the passenger seat, slamming the door behind him. "Go, go, go!" Allen gasped from the back seat, his breath coming in ragged bursts.

Jillian floored the accelerator, the car jerking forward as they sped away from the forest. The unsettling noises of the night faded into the distance.

"What happened?" Jared demanded, his voice tight as he glanced between Allen and the road ahead.

Allen shook his head, still trying to steady his breathing. "There are so many out there," he mumbled, the horror of what he had seen evident in his eyes. "I was trying to get the door for you, you had your hands full."

Silence fell over them, the terror of what lay in the woods becoming more than just a fear—it was a fact.

They pulled up to Allen's cabin, the quiet of the night a stark contrast to the chaos they had just escaped. Jared and Jillian helped Allen inside, the three of them moving as if in a daze. Once inside, they settled Allen onto the couch, his face pale and drawn from pain and exhaustion.

Jillian's voice trembled as she spoke, breaking the silence that had enveloped them. "What now?"

Allen took a deep breath, wincing slightly as he shifted on the couch. "We need to see what's on those cameras," his voice steady but low. There was no time to dwell on what had just happened—they needed answers.

Jared's hands shook as he set up the laptop, the images of the creature still fresh in his mind. The terror of the encounter clung to him, making his fingers tremble as he connected the cameras. He needed to focus, to push through the fear.

They gathered around the screen, the soft glow of the laptop casting eerie shadows on their faces. Allen pulled up the footage from the trail cameras, his heart pounding as the first clips played. At first, the footage showed the usual wildlife, moving silently through the night. But as the night deepened, the scene began to shift. Memories began flooding back—memories of the last time they had seen John alive.

The screen flickered, showing the pond under the cover of night, the water dark and still. John appeared in the frame, his flashlight beam cutting through the shadows. The eerie silence of the footage pulled them in.

What was he doing?

John's figure was tense, cautious, as he glanced back one last time before making his way around the pond. The darkness seemed to close in on him as he moved farther from the camera's view. Then, suddenly, he paused, his flashlight illuminating a figure emerging from the shadows.

The three of them held their breath watching the last time John was seen alive. Then a figure stepped into the light.

It was Victor.

DECEIT

"**THAT'S THE GUY** you're running against!" Jared exclaimed, pointing at the screen as the image of Victor flickered before disappearing. "He was talking about cleaning up this town. I saw him at the town hall."

The video cut out as the camera's battery died, leaving the room in heavy silence. Allen remained reserved, his mind racing as he processed what they had just seen.

"The camera was off when I found it," Jared sighed, frustration etched into his voice.

Jillian shook her head, disbelief washing over her. "So, you mean we didn't catch Ethan at all?"

"There are other cameras," Jared said, though the confidence in his voice had waned.

With their hearts pounding, they quickly loaded up the footage from the other two cameras. The air grew thick with tension as they watched the scenes unfold. The first camera revealed shadowy figures moving through the woods, circling as if they knew John was coming. Ethan appeared, pulling a hose from his truck just as John approached the tanker. They watched as Ethan turned the valve. The toxic sludge began to pour into the pond, the slow-moving poison flowing down the bank.

Then, abruptly, the footage cut off.

"Who are all these people?" Jared wondered aloud, his voice strained. "Who's allowing all this to happen?"

The tension in the room was palpable as they loaded the final camera, which had been aimed directly at the pond. The screen flickered to life, showing only wildlife—stray cats and dogs—drinking from the pond's edge, unaware of the poison they were consuming. Jillian's eyes narrowed as she glared at the screen, watching the animals lap up the toxic water.

"I need to get a water sample," Jillian insisted, determination lacing her words. "They're still dumping in that pond. I need to figure out what's really happening here."

"It won't do any good," Jared interjected, shaking his head. "I took them a sample, and the health department blew me off completely. They didn't even care."

Jillian's brow furrowed in thought. "Something isn't adding up," she murmured, her voice tinged with suspicion.

As the gravity of their findings settled over them, the room grew cold and quiet. The moonlight filtered through the windows. It cast eerie shadows that seemed to mirror the dark answers they had uncovered.

Meanwhile, across town, the tension was no less intense.

Ethan parked his truck in a deserted lot, the dim glow of a flickering neon sign splintering into jagged reflections on the pavement. The air was thick with the burnt scent of plastic and oil. A distant thunder hinted at an approaching storm. He walked to a dimly lit bar where Victor was waiting. The low hum of chatter from the other patrons added to the secrecy of their meeting.

Victor glanced up as Ethan approached, his expression tight with frustration. "You're late."

"Had to make sure I wasn't followed," Ethan replied, sliding into the seat across from him. His eyes darted around the bar, his unease barely concealed. "What's so urgent?"

Victor leaned in, lowering his voice to a harsh whisper. "Allen Boyd. He's becoming a real problem. We need to take him out of the picture before the election."

Ethan smirked, though a flicker of unease crossed his face. "I've been dumping in that pond for years. I knew Jared lived there ages ago. That's why I dumped there to begin with, he's no good. His neighbor came a knockin' and I told her it was nothing to worry about, all natural. Everything is natural ain't it? But Allen... he's going to be a tougher nut to crack.

"I'm putting money into that Water Treatment Center," Victor emphasized, bitterness creeping into his tone. "I had to work like a dog to get here. I'm not letting this slip away now. I want these men, solved, before the election."

Ethan nodded, the weight of the task settling heavily on his shoulders. "Leave Jared to me. I'll handle Allen. I want this tied up as much as you do."

Victor's eyes narrowed, his distrust evident. "You better. We can't afford any loose ends."

Ethan's phone buzzed, pulling his attention away. He glanced at the screen and stood up, slipping the phone back into his pocket. "I've got another pickup outside of town. When I get back, I'll take care of it. But remember, they know we are coming."

Victor watched as Ethan walked away, unease gnawing at him. The stakes were higher than ever, and the pressure was mounting. Outside, Ethan paused, glancing around to ensure no one was watching. His mind was already working through the plan—every detail had to be perfect, or everything would fall apart.

A raven cawed in the distance, its cry echoing through the still night air like an ominous warning. Ethan shivered, though he quickly dismissed the feeling. As he climbed into his truck, the unease lingered, a dark omen hanging over their plans.

REVELATIONS

THE NEXT MORNING, tension filled the car as Jillian, Allen, and Jared drove to the health department. They needed evidence, something tangible to bring this madness to an end. The rain fell steadily, a gray shroud of clouds hanging low over the town as they pulled into the parking lot.

"I'm going to get more than one vial to collect samples," Jillian said, her voice steady but underscored by urgency. "Keep an eye out." She got out of the car and sprinted through the rain to the building. Her eyes searched for anything unusual before she reached the door.

Inside, the health department was dimly lit, the flickering fluorescent lights casting an eerie glow over the room. Jillian approached the counter, where a disinterested man sat behind a thick pane of glass.

"Excuse me, hello?" she called, trying to keep her voice calm.

The man barely looked up, gesturing lazily toward the sign-in sheet. "Sign in," he grumbled, his tone indifferent.

Jillian's heart pounded as she scribbled her name on the sheet. "I'm Dr. Simons, a marine biologist from the coast. I need to collect a few samples from the area. Do you have any drug testing jars or something similar I can use?"

The man let out an audible sigh, his eyes rolling as he stood up. "One moment," he muttered, disappearing into the back.

As Jillian waited, her eyes darted around the room. A security camera in the corner caught her attention, and she felt a chill run down her spine. The man returned moments later with two vials, which he dropped onto the counter with a careless flick of his wrist, watching them roll.

"Here," he said curtly.

"Thank you," Jillian replied, catching the vials and hurrying back out to the car. The rain had lightened, but the sky remained a dreary gray as they drove toward the pond — a place that had become the epicenter of their investigation.

When they arrived, the rain had stopped, leaving the air crisp and clean. The trees stood tall and silent, their leaves still glistening with moisture. As they neared the pond, Jillian saw a raven at the water's edge. Its matted, dull feathers were a mess. It coughed and sneezed as it weakly pecked at the ground. The sight tugged at her heart, and she approached cautiously, her pulse quickening.

The raven's beak and belly were stained a sickly yellow, as if the toxic water had bleached its feathers. Gently, Jillian offered it some clean water from her bottle. The raven, too weak to fly away, shuffled closer and drank. Its dark, intelligent eyes met hers, and for a moment, it seemed to understand the kindness she offered. Jillian wiped the slimy coating from its beak, and the bird fluttered weakly into the trees, leaving her with a deep sense of foreboding.

With a deep breath, she collected the samples from the muck, her hands steady despite the unease gnawing at her. "We need to get these samples back to the lab," she murmured, standing up. "This could be the key to everything."

They drove straight to the EPA office, pulling into the lot next to a small black car. Jillian stepped out, the vial in hand, and sprinted inside. Her heart raced as she approached the front desk.

"I need to drop off this water sample for local testing," Jillian said, her voice calm but firm. "I've been conducting third-party research."

The clerk behind the desk looked up with a smirk, his eyes glinting with something dark. "Tannins, huh?

The water looks fine to me. Just some floating leaf debris, that's all." He set a piece of paper on the counter with a dismissive wave. "You can take this if you like."

Jillian's heart skipped a beat as she recognized him—he was one of the men she'd seen in the woods. Her blood ran cold as she realized the gravity of the situation. These weren't just random employees—they were part of the corruption she was fighting against.

Keeping her composure, she quickly pulled out her phone. "I'll just take a photo of it," she said, snapping pictures of the paper and, subtly, of the clerk's face. Another man emerged from the back room, and Jillian's stomach dropped. These were the men from the woods. A sense of dread tightened around her chest as she turned and hurried out of the building.

Back in the car, Jillian shared her discovery, her voice barely above a whisper. "Those were the people in the woods," she muttered, her eyes wide with fear.

They sat in the car, the weight of the situation sinking in as they eyed the last vial. "Let's take this sample to my lab in Salvo," Jillian urged, her voice tight with determination. "I have a feeling the people running the agency here are in on it."

As they started the car, a caw came from the trees above. They looked up to see an unkindness of ravens watching them, their dark eyes gleaming with an eerie intelligence. The birds seemed to be studying them, as if they knew more than they were letting on. As they drove away, a thick fog began to roll in, obscuring the road ahead.

Jared used the wipers to clear the windshield. His breath caught as he saw a shadowy figure in the trees. It moved with a predatory grace before vanishing into the mist.

"Ethan," Jared whispered, the name escaping his lips like a curse.

Jillian floored the accelerator, the car speeding down the road toward Salvo. The remaining vial had to make it to her lab—everything depended on it. But as they drove, Jillian's heart skipped a beat. In the rearview mirror, a tanker truck appeared, its massive form looming closer.

Jared confirmed her worst fear. "It's Ethan," he confirmed, his voice tense.

"Drive faster," Jillian urged, panic rising in her voice as the tanker truck's engine roared behind them.

The truck picked up speed, slamming into the back of their car with a bone-jarring impact. Jared struggled to keep control as the car fishtailed on the wet road...

BEHIND YOU

"HOLD ON!" Jared yelled, his knuckles white as he gripped the steering wheel. The tanker truck rammed into them again, harder this time. The car swerved wildly, tires screeching against the wet asphalt. Jillian felt the precious vial slip from her fingers, her heart stopping. If they lost it, everything they had fought for would be lost.

The fog around them thickened, turning the world outside into a blur of gray and fading outlines. Jillian frantically searched the floorboard for the vial. The tanker truck's headlights pierced the mist like two glowing eyes. With a deafening roar, the truck rammed them again, the impact sending the car lurching violently to the side. The sound of metal grinding against metal filled the air, a harsh reminder of how close they were to the edge.

"Jared, look out!" Jillian screamed as the road ahead twisted sharply.

Jared yanked the steering wheel, trying to keep the car from careening into the guardrail. The tires struggled for traction on the slick pavement, the car fishtailing dangerously. The tanker truck loomed closer, relentless.

Jillian's scream caught in her throat as they slammed into the guardrail, sparks flying as the metal barrier scraped against the side of the car. The truck, driven by Ethan in a blind rage, swerved to hit them but couldn't control its momentum. It burst through the guardrail, crashing into the embankment with a deafening roar. The truck's horn blared as the metal crumpled into the earth, the sound echoing in the mist.

Their car slid to a stop, the world suddenly eerily quiet except for the sound of their ragged breaths. Jared and Jillian exchanged a glance, shock and disbelief etched on their faces. They were alive, but the danger wasn't over.

Jared stumbled out of the car, his hands shaking as he dialed 911. "We're on Highway 4, just outside of town! We've been rammed off the road by a tanker truck! Please, hurry!" His voice trembled with urgency.

Suddenly, a cloud of ravens descended from the trees. Their caws filling the air with an awful, piercing noise. The birds swarmed around the wrecked truck, black feathers swirling in the fog. Ethan forced open the door of the semi and stumbled out. With his gun in hand.

Bang! Bang!

He fired into the mass of birds, but they only seemed to grow more frenzied, attacking him with a ferocity that made him scream in pain and anger.

"Get back in the car!" Jillian shouted, her voice barely audible over the cacophony of caws and gunshots.

They scrambled back into the vehicle, as a bullet hit their windshield. From the car they watched the surreal scene unfold. The ravens clawed and pecked at Ethan, their beaks tearing at his clothes and skin. He thrashed wildly, trying to fight them off, but the birds were relentless, driven by a primal fury.

Ethan's screams faded into gurgles as he collapsed to the ground, his body a dark mass beneath the flurry of wings. The distant wail of sirens grew louder, the flashing red and blue lights cutting through the fog as the police arrived on the scene. The officers hesitated, watching in stunned silence as the birds finished their assault.

"It's clear what happened here," one of the officers finally spoke, surveying the chaotic scene. He noted the caved-in rear bumper and the deep scratches along the side where the car had scraped the guardrail. "We'll include your damages in the report. I've never seen anything like this." Steam rose from the crumpled truck, now dotted with ravens perched on its twisted metal frame.

Jillian and Jared, shaken but unharmed, climbed back into their car. It was banged up but still running. Adrenaline still coursed through their veins, but a heavy silence hung between them. Ethan getting taken down didn't mean their job was over.

Upon arriving at the aquarium, the familiar smell of saltwater and the soft hum of the tanks greeted them. Jillian led the way to her lab, her steps purposeful, driven by the condition of the raven she had seen.

She carefully set the vial on the lab table and began her analysis, her hands steady as she worked through the testing procedures. Jared and Allen watched in tense silence, the room filled with the quiet hum of equipment and the occasional beep of a monitor.

As the results came in, Jillian's eyes widened in shock. "There's formaldehyde in it," she whispered, her voice barely more than a breath. "Yes, there are many other chemicals, but this one is specific. This one isn't common like the others."

Jared leaned in, his face pale. "Formaldehyde? In the pond? How the hell did it get in there?"

"Victor," Allen rasped, his voice weak but determined. "He owns Elmhurst's Funeral Home. I bet he hired Ethan to cut costs, to dump the chemicals instead of disposing of them properly. It's carcinogenic, meaning it causes cancer."

Jillian's mind raced, the pieces of the puzzle finally coming together. "We need to expose this. If this gets out, it could bring down everyone involved."

"But how do we do that?" Jared asked, his voice laced with urgency and doubt. "They've covered their tracks so well. And now Ethan's gone—who knows what Victor will do next?"

Jillian looked at the results in her hands, then at Jared and Allen. She realized that there weren't any demons left in hell; they had all crawled out of the pond. Determination hardened in her gaze. "We go public. We take this to the media, the authorities, whoever will listen. We can't let them get away with this."

Allen nodded slowly, a grim smile tugging at the corner of his mouth. "Let's bring them down."

THE RECKONING

THEY WERE HEADING into war, and they knew it. Every breath was labored, every heartbeat like a drum they could feel in their chests. Jillian gripped the steering wheel, the pressure almost unbearable. The town's once-familiar streets now felt foreign. An eerie silence hung in the air, the tar scarring the deserted asphalt. It was as if the town itself knew another battle was on the horizon.

Ahead, a banner framed the town square, promising "important updates about the town's future," with Victor's name plastered across it like a brand. It wasn't just a banner; it was a bold invitation. Jillian's gaze hardened.

"We need to be there," she said, her voice steady. Her eyes flicked to Allen, who nodded grimly, his crutches resting against the dash. They were all in this together, and there was no turning back now.

The next day, the town hall was a sea of faces, tension rippling through the crowd like a physical force. The air buzzed with whispers, sharp glances following Jillian as she helped Allen through the crowd. Jillian could feel it—eyes on her, distrust swirling around them. Victor had worked hard to poison the minds of the crowd, and it showed in every hostile stare. But she kept moving, Allen by her side, the weight of the truth propelling them forward.

Victor stepped onto the stage, his presence commanding, almost smug. He scanned the crowd but didn't see Jared. The crowd hushed instantly, his charisma palpable. He wore a smile that didn't reach his eyes, the kind of grin that made your skin crawl.

"My fellow citizens," he began, his voice smooth and dripping with practiced charm. "We stand on the brink of a brighter future, one that promises safety and prosperity for us all."

He paused, letting the words settle, letting the crowd soak in his lies. Then, his tone shifted, darkening like a cloud before a storm.

"But," he continued, raising a newspaper high above his head, "not everyone shares our vision." The crowd murmured, uneasy. Victor held up the newspaper. The headline blared: *Failing Businessman Causes Drunk Driving Accident.* A calculated jab at Allen, a man who had once been the town's rock.

"Where's Allen been?" Victor sneered, his voice sharp as a blade. "We've all seen his store shut down.

He's been reckless—caused an accident that could've killed someone. What kind of man is that? And now he's bringing outsiders to take over our town? Can you trust a man like this with our future, much less military-grade weapons?"

The crowd erupted in agreement, the sound crashing over them like a wave. Jillian's heart clenched as she glanced at Allen. His face was pale, his shoulders slumped under the weight of the partial truth in Victor's words. A team of security guards lined the stage, their loyalty clear.

Victor's grin widened. He thrived on the chaos, on the power he held over them. "We trusted him," he declared, his voice rising with each word. "But while we work to build a better future, Allen is out there destroying everything we've built."

Jillian's pulse quickened. This was their moment— the truth had to come out now, or they would lose everything. She nudged Allen gently, urging him forward. He rose, his crutches clicking against the pavement as he limped toward the stage. Every eye followed his slow ascent, the crowd's anger simmering just beneath the surface.

When Allen reached the microphone, the crowd grew tense, dismissive. A few scattered boos greeted him.

"Accidents happen," Allen began, his voice steady but strained. "But what Victor hasn't told you is that I wasn't drunk. I was poisoned. Victor has been dumping toxic chemicals into the very water we drink."

A wave of disbelief rippled through the crowd. Before they could react, Jillian stepped forward, her hand raised. A small vial glinted under the fluorescent lights of the hall.

"This," she announced, her voice clear and strong, "is untreated formaldehyde. I found it in the pond water here."

She held up a report, its bold letters standing out for all to see. "Here are the findings—untreated formaldehyde. The same chemical used in funeral homes." Her eyes scanned the crowd. The evidence shifted the mood, turning the crowd's confusion into something far more dangerous: anger and outrage.

"We've got more," Jillian continued, her heart pounding. She pulled out images—printouts from trail camera footage. Screenshots of the truck dumping waste into the pond. Another image of Victor himself, standing by the tanker near the pond. The crowd erupted again, but this time, the anger wasn't aimed at Allen. It was turning, slowly, on Victor.

Victor's confident facade cracked. His eyes darted, wild and desperate, searching for an exit, but none came. Allen stepped forward again, his voice growing stronger, louder.

"Talk is cheap," he said firmly into the microphone, his eyes locked on Victor. "You've poisoned this town for your own gain. You've betrayed us all."

Victor's voice wavered, his desperation clawing at him. "This is all lies! A setup! That's not me!"

But his words were drowned out by the rising roar of the crowd. Someone shouted, "Arrest him!" and the cry spread like wildfire. The security guards, once loyal to Victor, exchanged uncertain glances, their resolve wavering.

"You want truth?" Allen announced. "Here's your truth!"

Then the doors to the town hall suddenly blew open with a deafening crash, and the room plunged into chaos.

TAKE HIM DOWN

THE INTENSE bang echoed through the hall. The crowd jerked toward the noise, the tension in the air thickening with dust and confusion. Jared stood at the back of the room, his broad frame silhouetted against the blinding light outside. He pushed a large metal cage through the doorway, its wheels screeching on the floor. Inside, a creature thrashed violently. Its skin was a grotesque patchwork of scabs and fur, as if nature itself had rejected it.

Gasps rippled through the crowd, then horror set in. This was no ordinary animal.

"This is what it does!" Jared's voice boomed over the rising chaos, cutting through the panic. "This is what this illegal dumping is doing to our animals, to our town!"

The collective gasp turned into a roar. Fear and fury swirled together as the townspeople saw the mutated creature up close. It had once been a stray dog, a familiar face on these streets, but now it was something monstrous. Teeth bared, eyes wild, it snarled, lunging against the bars of the cage.

Victor, standing near the stage, froze for a moment. Jared, towering behind the cage, blocked the only exit. The creature's rabid snapping made escape impossible.

Victor lunged toward the door, but Jared was quicker, sliding the cage into his path. The creature snarled, thrashing violently against the bars, its savage barks echoing like thunder. Victor stumbled back, his face pale, realizing escape was impossible.

"This ends now," Jared growled, his voice sending finality through the room.

Victor's composure shattered. His face twisted in panic, his desperation erratic. "This is all a setup!" he screamed, his voice cracking as he flailed for control. "They're framing me! These are all lies!"

But the crowd had heard enough. They surged forward, their anger tangible, their shouts growing louder, more dangerous. People pushed and jostled, their fury building like a storm. The stage security guards hesitated, exchanging nervous glances. Their loyalty to Victor was wavering.

"Can you explain the formaldehyde in the pond?" Allen's voice rang out from the stage, steady and unyielding amidst the growing chaos. "Can you explain the photos, the reports—this creature!?"

Victor's eyes darkened, his fear morphing into something uglier—rage. "You can't turn this town against me! I've done more for this place than any of you!"

A trembling voice pierced the noise—a frail, elderly woman standing near the front. Her voice shook with emotion. "Victor! You poisoned our pets... our children! How could you?"

The crowd exploded. Rage boiled over, the townspeople no longer able to hold back their fury. A book flew through the air, striking Victor squarely in the face. He stumbled, clutching his nose as blood dripped between his fingers. The chant began—soft at first, but quickly growing louder, more forceful—a unified cry for justice: "Arrest him! Arrest him!"

The police rushed into the building around Jared, closing in on Victor. They grabbed him, throwing him to the ground. His hands flailed helplessly, but it was over. His reign of power had crumbled. The crowd watched as they restrained him. He spewed venomous words, glaring with hatred in his eyes.

"You'll pay for this," Victor hissed to Jillian, his words like poison through gritted teeth. "You'll all pay."

Jillian stepped forward, holding the vial of formaldehyde high for everyone to see. Her voice, though shaky with emotion, was clear. "This isn't just about what you've done to us," she said, her voice full of purpose and passion. "It's about everyone you've hurt—our animals, our water, and our children."

Victor glared up at her, but there was nothing left for him now. The police dragged him away, his words echoing in the silent room.

As the crowd began to disperse, the sharp crack of gunfire pierced the tense air, freezing everyone in place. For a moment, time seemed to stand still, the deafening echo of the shots bouncing off the walls.

ECHOES

THE ONCE-RAUCOUS crowd fell into a tense, uneasy silence. The energy of their anger had dissipated, replaced by a chilling fear that hung thick in the air. Eyes darted to the slightly ajar double doors. The last rays of the setting sun cast long, beams of light into the dimly lit hall.

Jillian's breath caught in her throat as she instinctively stepped closer to Jared. But it was Allen who moved first, his soldier's instincts kicking in despite his injuries. "Everyone stay down!" Allen shouted, his voice authoritative, cutting through the air. He hobbled forward on his crutches, his voice steady yet filled with urgency as he gestured for the crowd to stay back. "Stay inside. Don't move," he ordered, his tone leaving no room for argument.

Jillian hesitated only for a moment before following Allen, with Jared close behind. The cool evening air hit them as they stepped outside, the wind biting at their skin. The faint scent of gunpowder lingered in the air, mingling with a familiar chemical smell that sent a shiver down their spines. Then, an unmistakable metallic tang reached their nostrils.

In the distance, a group of police officers stood in a tight circle, their faces pale under the dying light of the day. Radio chatter crackled through the air, punctuated by urgent calls for an ambulance.

The rhythmic click of Allen's crutches on the pavement drew the officers' attention as the trio approached. "What happened?" Allen called out, his voice cutting through the tension like a knife.

One of the officers turned to face them, his expression grave, his eyes betraying the gravity of the situation. "Return inside," he said quietly, though the weight in his tone was impossible to ignore. "Victor tried to escape. A gun went off..."

Jillian's heart raced, her eyes wide with shock. "And?" she pressed, her voice trembling with a mix of disbelief and dread.

The officer hesitated for a moment, glancing at the body sprawled on the pavement a few feet away. Victor's lifeless body lay there, hands still cuffed. He wasn't going to make it. "He reached for my gun and a shot went off," the officer continued, his voice heavy. "We had no choice... he was trying to get away. Please, stay back."

A flood of conflicting emotions washed over Jillian. Jail confines the body, but death imprisons the soul, ending all chance for change. Victor couldn't even talk now, evil was just out there running free. Jillian felt relief that Victor was no longer a threat, but a deep unease gnawed at her. Something didn't feel right.

As the officers began to secure the scene, something caught Jared's attention. He narrowed his eyes, focusing on Victor's still-cuffed hands. A frown creased his brow. How had Victor managed to grab a gun while restrained? The scenario didn't add up. His instincts screamed that something was off.

Then, the distant sound of a car door slamming pulled Jared's gaze away from the scene. He spotted a small black car pulling away from the curb, its tires screeching as it sped down the street, disappearing into the twilight. The knot in Jared's stomach tightened. If Victor had been restrained, what gun did he fire?

LOOSE ENDS

VICTOR'S END had left them with more questions than answers. His final moments weren't a conclusion but a lead—a thread that, if pulled, might lead them to the root of the problem.

Jared leaned closer to Allen, his voice low and tinged with urgency. "This isn't over," he whispered. "We need to get out of here."

Allen's eyes narrowed, darkening with the realization that there was more at play than what they had witnessed. "Let's head back to my store," he suggested, his tone leaving no room for debate. "We'll be safer there, and we can figure out our next move."

They said nothing more. The three turned from the unsettling sight and quickly retreated to Allen's car. An unease settled in their chests as they drove through the deserted streets. The sun sank below the horizon, and the night swallowed the last of the daylight.

"Pull around back," Allen instructed, his voice steady despite the turmoil inside him. As they parked, he fumbled with his keys, his hands trembling slightly, a residue of adrenaline still coursing through him. He managed to unlock the door and usher them inside. The store was dimly lit, the air heavy with a musky scent along with old metal. No one had stepped foot inside for over a week, but it was a sanctuary — a place where they could think and plan.

Allen led the way into the store. Jared stood nearby, his gaze fixed on the windows, scanning the street for any sign of movement. The soft glow of the streetlight filtered through the window, tracing faint patterns across the room.

"So, you think the police are in on it?" Jillian asked, her voice barely above a whisper. "This whole town knew Victor. It could have been anyone, couldn't it? He could have tried to reach for the gun in handcuffs. I've seen footage of people trying."

Allen nodded slowly, his brow furrowed in thought. "Everyone running is being hunted. There must be someone else behind this — a missing piece we haven't found yet."

He glanced around the store, the familiar sight of camo jackets, old rubber gas masks, and even a few weapons offering a strange sense of comfort. They had everything they needed to defend themselves, but against what? The enemy was still out there, hidden just out of view, waiting in the places where light dared not reach.

Jared's eyes narrowed as his mind drifted back to the people at the EPA. "It had to be one of them, right? They've been too involved from the start."

Allen called them into a small room in the back, where a large war table was set up, covered with maps and equipment. Jillian spread out the printouts of the men they had seen in the woods, their faces illuminated by the dim light. The reports, the footage—they all pointed to the same place.

"All those people who were in the woods," Jared said, tapping the table, "they all work at the EPA office."

Jillian leaned in, her heart pounding as she stared at the evidence. "We need to do something. We need to get this footage to the authorities, let the police identify them."

Allen shook his head, his expression grim. "We can't trust the local police. Not after what we've seen. Victor had connections all over this town. It could be anyone."

"Victor might have been the face of this," Allen continued, his voice steady. "But, there's someone else behind it—someone who's still out there." Let's go see this treatment plant he was building. We need to find them before they make their next move."

Jared's suspicions about what Victor had been brewing for a while, and now it seemed more justified than ever. "The EPA has been too involved from the beginning. We need to see what's been going on."

Jillian's anxiety grew, the weight of the situation pressing down on her. "We can't do this alone. We should turn over the footage to the FBI, or someone outside this town. If we try to take them down ourselves, we'll be putting ourselves in even more danger."

Allen remained resolute. "What if the authorities are compromised? If we hand this over and they're part of the conspiracy, we'll be signing our own death warrants. No, we need to gather more evidence—something undeniable—then make it public before it's too late."

Jared nodded, agreeing with the need for caution. "We have to be smart about this. If an officer is involved, it'll come out in the investigation. We just need to make sure the evidence is strong enough that they can't cover it up."

With the plan set, they knew they were on the brink of something much bigger than they had anticipated. The risks were higher than ever, but there was no turning back now. With a nod, the three of them began gathering gear—flashlights, night vision goggles, anything that might help them in what lay ahead. They were already targets; hesitation could mean death.

Under the cover of darkness, they arrived near Victor's Water Treatment building. The sterile structure loomed against the night sky like a fortress of secrets. The grass was perfectly manicured, and the metal doors were solid, without windows. It was the kind of place that whispered lies in the dark.

Taking up positions in the woods nearby, they used binoculars to surveil the building. Each minute stretched into an eternity as they watched for any sign of life.

As the moon reached its peak, two figures emerged from the building. Jared's heart skipped a beat as he recognized them—Darrel Swain, the head of the EPA, was there. His mind raced as he tried to piece together what they could be discussing. Why would the head of the EPA be here at this place, after hours?

More people joined them as the group filed in for the meeting. The resemblance to the group they had seen in the woods was striking—these were the same men. A garage door opened, revealing a large building. It wasn't a treatment center, nor was it empty. Those had been lies all along. Inside, truck after truck filled the space. This wasn't a treatment center at all. They could collect chemicals from any facility and dump them in the night. Swain was giving them a tour of the new tanker trucks, freshly polished and ready for transport. Then, all three froze as a bandaged man hopped out of the truck—Ethan.

"Did you get enough photos?" Jared whispered, his voice tight with tension. "We need to get out of here."

They watched in disbelief as Ethan, alive and back to work, supervised the new garage. He was already resuming the operation they had thought they had disrupted. They quickly packed up and retreated with the last of the evidence to Allen's Military Surplus Store.

As they drove away, Jillian glanced back. She watched Darrel Swain slip into the driver's seat of his black car. His features obscured by the tinted windows. Swain had spotted them.

CONFRONTED

"**ARE YOU COMING?**" Jillian whispered urgently, glancing back at Jared, who was still glued to his binoculars. He couldn't tear his eyes away from the scene—Ethan was alive. Darrel Swain, the man they had crossed paths with before, was hiding in plain sight. He could have been the one that shot Victor at the townhall meeting. The thought that someone they had trusted could be working against them was a chilling reminder of just how deep the corruption ran. Who better to lead John into the woods at night? They all worked together.

Jared's thoughts raced, his mind a whirlwind of fear and determination. Ethan knew them—knew their tactics, their weaknesses. If he was leading the charge against them, they were in grave danger. This wasn't just business anymore; it was personal. And Ethan wouldn't stop until they were silenced for good.

"We have to assume he's coming after us," Jared insisted, his voice edged with grim determination. "And he knows the vehicles. We still haven't gotten the car fixed; it stands out. We're sitting ducks."

They climbed back into the car, the tension thick in the air as they sped back to the store. The woods surrounding them were eerily silent. As they arrived, Jared joined Jillian at the back of the store, the reality of their situation pressing down on them like a weight.

"You okay?" Jared asked, his voice softening as he looked at her, concern etched on his face.

She nodded, though her heart was pounding. "I just... I didn't expect this. I think I've seen that black car before. I saw that guy when I dropped the sample vial off at the EPA."

"His name is Darrel Swain," Jared confirmed, his tone filled with a mix of anger and disbelief. "He interviewed me and Allen about the toxic pond. He was working with John. He knew all along," his mind raced to piece everything together, the puzzle taking on a darker shape.

Before Jillian could respond, large headlights appeared down the road. Engines revved, filling the air with a low growl. As it grew louder, it was an unmistakable rumble of several vehicles approaching. The trio exchanged a tense look, each of them knowing what was coming.

"Ethan," Allen grunted, his voice cold and steady.

Jared moved to the window, watching as the headlights cut through the darkness, casting long, menacing shadows. Amidst the vehicles, one stood out—the tanker truck. It was the centerpiece of the convoy, like a harbinger of doom.

"They brought the tanker," Jared muttered, his stomach twisting with fear and fury.

Jillian's breath hitched as she thought about what could be inside the truck. That tanker could wipe them all off the map, and Ethan wouldn't hesitate to do it. They were trapped, surrounded by enemies who knew enough to be dangerous.

"I'm calling the police," Jillian decided, her voice urgent. She slipped into the bathroom to make the call, praying for timely help.

Outside, the sound of footsteps and shouted orders echoed through the night as the attackers began to move in, their intent clear and deadly. Jared and Allen braced themselves, Allen clutching a grenade in his hand, his grip tight and steady.

"Stay low, stay quiet," Jared whispered to Allen. His eyes locked on the glass doors at the front of the store, every muscle in his body tensed for the inevitable.

But the calm was shattered in an instant. "Get down!" Jared yelled as a black car barreled through the parking lot, its tires screeching as it came to a halt. Allen knelt behind a rack of uniforms, while Jared hit the floor, heart pounding.

The glass doors exploded inward as bullets tore through the night. The stillness was shattered by a deafening gunfire. The attackers unleashed a relentless barrage of bullets. They ripped through the wooden walls and sent splinters flying in every direction.

The noise was overwhelming, the air thick with the smell of gunpowder. Jared's heart raced as he returned fire, each shot a desperate attempt to keep the attackers at bay. But he knew they were outnumbered and outgunned.

Then, through the chaos, Jared caught sight of Ethan, standing by the tanker truck, a cruel smile playing on his lips. He was watching them, reveling in the destruction, knowing that he held all the cards. The sight of him filled Jared with a cold fury. This was the man who had orchestrated everything, who had pushed them to the brink.

As the gunfire paused momentarily, Jared's eyes drifted over to Allen. He was crouched low, his face a grimace of determination.

"Stay here!" Allen grunted, his tone leaving no room for argument. There was a fire in his eyes.

Jared was about to counter when a pungent, sickly smell began to seep into the store. His eyes widened in horror as he realized what was happening—they had begun draining the tanker into the store. The foul liquid spread across the floor, carrying with it the threat of something far worse.

"Allen!" Jared voiced, fear gripping his heart. But it was too late. Allen was already moving. His crutches clattered against the floor as he hurried to the door, ready to do whatever it took. He needed to get the grenade outside, to end this once and for all.

As the toxic sludge inched closer, the true scale of the threat became clear. Ethan wasn't going to let them escape this time.

INFERNO

THE CHEMICAL STENCH from the tanker filled the air. It stung Jillian's eyes and made it nearly impossible to breathe. The realization hit her like a freight train. They were pumping something directly into the store. If they didn't act quickly, there would be nothing left to save.

Allen slipped and collapsed in the sludge as Jared went after him. Jillian rushed over, seeing the fear in their eyes. Jared had to pull Allen to safety, to get him out of this toxic muck before it ignited. Jared's voice cut through the rising panic. "They're draining something into the store!" he shouted, his voice laced with desperation. "We've got to get out of here!"

Jillian's heart raced as she dropped her phone, the urgency of the situation overriding everything else. The police were on their way, but they were still minutes out—minutes they didn't have.

Silently she watched as Jared pulled Allen to the back of the store.

Jared's eyes widened as he understood what she was about to do. "Out the back," he directed, his voice tight with urgency. Jared was the only one who could move Allen; this chance was all they had.

Jillian took a deep breath, steeling herself for what needed to be done. She pulled the grenade from Allen's hand, its cold weight reassuring in her grasp. This had to work.

Finally out in the back of the store, a flame ignited in the front of the store. He tossed Allen a gun and began firing shots out of the building. The men outside returned fire, their focus drawn to the flashes coming from inside the store. The liquid continued to seep in, the fumes growing stronger and more suffocating with each passing second.

Crouching low, Jillian kept to the shadows as she made her way around the building. The tanker loomed large in the parking lot. She could see Ethan directing his men with ruthless precision. She could see the satisfaction through the bandages on his face. The group was unaware she was creeping upon them.

Rounding the edge of the store, her fingers tightened around the grenade. Just a few feet from the tanker, she pulled the pin. Her breath caught as she hurled the grenade with all her strength. The world seemed to slow as she watched it arc through the air, her heart pounding in her throat. The metallic clang as it struck the tanker echoed in her ears, followed by a split second of silence that felt like an eternity.

Then, with a deafening roar, the grenade detonated.

The explosion was instantaneous and overwhelming. A massive fireball erupted from the tanker, tearing through the night. The force of the blast knocked Jillian off her feet, sending her crashing around the side of the store. Debris flew in every direction from the tanker.

Flames shot into the sky, painting the night with an eerie, hellish glow. The store's windows shattered, glass spraying inward as the building shook from the explosion.

Darrel, standing too close to the tanker, was caught in the heart of the blast. The shockwave hit him with brutal force, hurling him through the air like a ragdoll. He slammed into the side of the brick building.

The men near Darrel fared no better. Some were thrown by the initial blast, finding rest as they fell from the sky. Others were caught in the searing heat as the flames swallowed them whole. There were no survivors, except for one.

The force of the blast splintered a massive tree near the road, its trunk cracking under the pressure. With a groaning creak, the tree began to fall. Its enormous weight pulling it down directly toward where Ethan lay, burnt and stunned on the ground.

Ethan looked up just in time to see the tree hurtling toward him. With a deadly crunch, its weight ended the threat he posed once and for all.

Jillian staggered to her feet, her body aching, but the store's wall had deflected the blast from her. For a moment, all she could do was stand there, dazed by the intensity of what had just happened. The realization settled in—she had done it. But at what cost?

Jillian watched the flames consume the front of the store. The chemicals that had seeped inside were fueling the fire.

ASHES

THE NIGHT AIR was thick with the scent of smoke and splintered wood. Jillian stood beside the wreckage of the tanker truck. Police lights flickered in the distance, cutting through the haze as they clawed their way through the thick smoke. The massive tree that had once towered over the road was now reduced to a tangled heap of burning branches. The immediate danger had passed, but the store—Allen's sanctuary—lay in ruins.

From the smoky debris, Jared emerged, supporting Allen over his shoulders. They were battered, their clothes torn and faces smudged with soot, but they were alive. Their sight stirred something deep within Jillian. She felt a fierce gratitude and relief that they had survived the night.

The sun rose slowly over Elmhurst, casting a soft golden light across the town that had endured so much darkness. A yellow-bellied raven perched atop a charred branch. It watched as smoke continued to rise over the town. The nightmare that had gripped the community was finally over, but the scars it left behind would take time to heal. As the morning light bathed the streets, people emerged from their homes. They were cautious and uncertain, but with a growing sense of hope.

As word spread of the events that had unfolded overnight, people began to gather. The store was destroyed, but Allen, Jared and Jillian were still standing. The community gathered, slowly. They offered their hands to help rebuild what was lost. They had lost so much. But, they had gained something too. They now knew their strength, their resilience, and their bond.

Burns caused Jared to be rushed to the hospital. The blast had made him get covered in the strange chemical. Jared had been their protector, their hero, and now it was her turn to protect him.

Hours passed in a blur of activity and worry as the doctor and his team worked to stabilize Jared. The poison running through his system was still present. Jillian stayed by his side, her hand never leaving his, her mind replaying the events of the last few days over and over.

Finally, the doctor emerged from the clinic's small operating room. His face showed exhaustion and relief. "He's stable," he smiled, his voice soft but steady. "He's not out of the woods yet, but he's going to make it."

The doctor smiled gently, placing a reassuring hand on Jillian's shoulder. "He's a fighter," he assured. "But he's going to need time to recover. You both will."

Jillian nodded, her gaze drifting back to the door behind which Jared lay. She knew the doctor was right—this was just the beginning of their journey to recovery. But for the first time in what felt like forever, she allowed herself to believe that they would get there.

The days that followed were filled with a quiet sense of renewal. The town began to rebuild, the poisoned pond at the heart of it all slowly returning to life as the last remnants of the chemicals were cleared away. The townspeople, once divided and afraid, united. Their shared trauma and a hope for a better future brought them together. It was found that the men planned to fake a tanker accident into the store. But, it didn't work out that way in the end.

Jillian spent most of her time at the clinic, keeping vigil at Jared's bedside. His recovery was slow but steady. Each day, he grew a little stronger, his spirit as indomitable as ever. In quiet moments, their talks held an unspoken understanding. It was of all they had endured and the bond that had formed between them. The wildlife would take time to heal, but so would they.

One evening, the sun set over the town. It cast a warm, golden glow through the clinic's windows. Jillian sat beside Jared, her hand in his. He was awake, his color much improved, though he still tired easily. The room was quiet, the only sound the soft hum of the clinic's equipment.

"You know," Jared mentioned, his voice rough but steady, "I never thought I'd make it out of this little town. You saved me, Jillian. You saved all of us."

Jillian's eyes filled with tears as she shook her head. "I couldn't have done it without you," she whispered. "You're the hero, Jared. You always have been. I didn't know how this was happening."

Jared looked into her eyes, his expression serious. "I'm not a hero," he spoke quietly. "I'm just a man that decided to do something myself. The real heroes are the people who fight everyday even when they don't want to. The people who refused to give up on each other."

Jillian felt a lump form in her throat, her emotions overwhelming her. She wanted to argue, to tell him that he was wrong. To tell him that he was more than just a man who had done what was necessary. But the words wouldn't come. Instead, she leaned forward, pressing a gentle kiss to his forehead.

"You'll always be a hero to me," she added softly, her voice trembling with the depth of her feelings.

Jared closed his eyes, a peaceful smile on his lips as he drifted back to sleep. Jillian stayed by his side, her heart full of love and gratitude, knowing that whatever the future held, they would face it together.

~ Years Later ~

The sun was warm on the little girl's skin as she walked through the sunlit grass, her small hand clutching a bright dandelion she had picked along the way. The grass was soft under her feet. The morning light danced on her auburn hair. She walked to a spot where the sun filtered perfectly through the trees.

Jillian smiled, watching her daughter. She had something to share with her daddy.

"Mom told me a story today about how you cleaned up the world and saved us," she began, her voice sweet and clear in the still morning air. "She said the discoloration in my skin is all that's left of the bad stuff."

The girl looked down at her feet, studying the patches of light and dark on her skin—her Vitiligo, her mother called it. She didn't mind it so much. It made her feel special, connected to her father, Jared.

With a small, determined smile, the girl reached into her pocket and pulled out a piece of paper, carefully unfolding it. "I wrote you a poem, Daddy," her voice soft. "I hope you like it."

She began to read:

> I really love you, Daddy.
> I think of you every day,
> And I hope I'm as brave as you.
> That when the monsters come again,
> I'll chase them far away.

The girl's voice wavered slightly as she finished the poem, but she smiled, proud of the words she had written. With a gentle hand, she placed the dandelion on the gravestone, her small fingers lingering on the cold stone.

"I love you, Daddy," she whispered, her small voice breaking the morning stillness. Her eyes shimmered with tears she didn't fully understand. "I'll always be brave, just like you."

As the girl stood up, a gentle breeze swept through the graveyard, causing the dandelion's petals to wave. They danced and fluttered, a golden echo of her father's spirit. She felt a wave of warmth wash over her, a quiet, reassuring presence. It was him. Smiling softly, she turned and began to walk back towards the path, carrying the sense of peace with her.

From a short distance, Jillian watched her daughter. Her heart swelled with a mixture of love and pride, a single tear sliding down her cheek. The dandelion, was waving goodbye. And his little girl was waving back. A silent tribute to the man who had given everything to make sure they didn't have to worry about the monsters. Jared's strength and courage lived on in their daughter, and Jillian knew she would be all right.

As the girl glanced back one last time, the sunlight bathed the gravestone in a warm, golden light. They rays illuminating the words: "Jared Owens - Beloved Father and Fierce Friend." Jillian felt a profound sense of peace. Despite all the pain and loss, Jared's love had woven a bond that could never be broken.

Taking her daughter's hand, Jillian walked down the path, away from the graveyard and into the future. They didn't know what lay ahead, but they would face it together, guided by the memory of Jared Owens—his bravery, his love, and the legacy he left behind.

The sun continued to rise, casting its light over Elmhurst. It was a new day, a new horizon. The town, once shadowed by fear and uncertainty, now stood resilient and united. Those who knew how bad it used to be were inspired by Jared. He made the ultimate sacrifice so that others could have a better life.

As Jillian and her daughter moved forward, hand in hand, they carried with them the knowledge that love endures beyond all things. In the hearts of those who remembered, Jared Owens would live forever.

Thank you for walking this journey with us. You've been through an intense adventure, and while Jared's journey has come to an end, the world of Pond Water still pulses with life, love, and untold secrets.

What about the people Jared left behind? Characters like Allen or his daughter Eithwin?

What if I told you there's been a hidden story woven through every chapter, waiting to be revealed? A thread that leads to Eithwin—holding the key to the next chapter, and perhaps even more.

Brenda thrives on your encouragement and support. If you've enjoyed this story, let her know by responding to her videos on social media. She loves writing, but it's your feedback that truly inspires her to keep going.

Your support has been my strength and inspiration. As long as I can write, I hope these stories make the world better

Your support has
been my strength and
inspiration. As long
as I can write, I
hope these stories
make the world better

~ Brenda FireEagle Biddix

THE SILENT STORY

Like its predecessor, this book comes with a gentle reminder. While the narrative weaves fiction, it's rooted in truths that are as unsettling as they are real.

This photo shows the old building that inspired this story. This building is no longer a funeral home. In 1993, the building changed, but its history remains. The embalming waste would drain from this pipe you can see on the outside of the building, flowing directly into a river that runs next to the elementary school. The river is connected to a public park and a flourishing campground. People still fish and swim in these waters, but most will never learn its history.

These are aerial and satellite views. They show the creek behind the funeral home. The creek flows through the trees into the town's river. These images show the connection to the main waterway.

Funeral Home shown in bottom left. River top Right.

VISIT
RianMileti.com

JOIN THE CONVERSATION

AHOY THERE, FANTASTIC READER OF POND WATER GENESIS! Whether you found it utterly unputdownable or it was not your cup of tea, your thoughts matter to us! Dive into a conversation with us by dropping a quick review on Amazon and/or Goodreads. And why stop there? Splash the word on TikTok too and there is a good chance we will respond! Make some waves! We are listening carefully and can't wait to soak in your insights. Plus, we adore sharing standout reviews with our awesome social media following.

http://www.RianMileti.com

Made in the USA
Columbia, SC
08 October 2024

43279934R00059